P9-AOI-325

Henry Holt and Company, *Publishers since 1866*
Henry Holt® is a registered trademark of Macmillan Publishing Group, LLC
120 Broadway, New York, NY 10271 • fiercereads.com

FLAMER. Copyright © 2020 by Mike Curato.
All rights reserved.

Library of Congress Cataloging-in-Publication Data is available.

Our books may be purchased in bulk for promotional, educational, or business use. Please
contact your local bookseller or the Macmillan Corporate and Premium Sales Department at
(800) 221-7945 ext. 5442 or by email at MacmillanSpecialMarkets@macmillan.com.

First edition, 2020 / Designed by Mallory Grigg and Colleen AF Venable
This book was made with black colored pencil and ink washes on bristol paper.
Printed in China by 1010 Printing International Limited, North Point, Hong Kong

ISBN 978-1-62779-641-5 (hardcover)
10 9 8 7 6 5 4 3 2 1

ISBN 978-1-250-75614-5 (paperback)
10 9 8 7 6 5 4 3 2 1

SATURDAY

AIDEN!!!

Huh?

Oh! CRAP!

Put that out before you burn the whole damn camp down!

FLAMER

MIKE CURATO

HENRY HOLT AND COMPANY
NEW YORK

GODWINBOOKS

My name is Aiden Navarro, and I am fourteen years old, and if it weren't for this stupid campfire, I'd still be daydreaming. But I guess I'm back in reality, so here's the ugly truth. I just cleared 5'6" and have been trying my best to make it to 5'7", despite my pediatrician.

Come on, Aiden, stand straight.

I AM!

Come on, you can do better than that.

erg

Sigh. Okay, just five-six.

Doctor Reyes also likes to point out how I'm fat.

well, maybe not fat. "overweight."

still sounds like "fat" to me.

Also, I've been wearing the same uniform every day for almost a decade. I've recently been informed that I don't know how to dress myself, but I think it's all a matter of opinion.

Catholic School Uniform

Everyday Look

collar shirt

plaid tie

sweater

turtlenecks are cool... right?

handy fanny pack

slacks (ugh)

comfy sweat shorts

dress shoes

these sneakers were on sale

At least I have this summer to have a break from school. This fall may be a fresh start, but it feels more like a prison transfer to me.

I like scouting. I guess some of the guys tease me a bit, but nothing nearly as bad as the jerks at St. Michael's.

And I love summer camp, mostly because I get a break from my parents yelling at each other. It's peaceful out in the woods.

Everything is so quiet.

NAVARRO!

...Except when it's not.

Rob Niccolo is my patrol leader, and I'm his assistant. He, Bobby McGuire, Mark Jones, Ryan Polowski, Elias Schaefer, David Green, and I make up the Flaming Arrow patrol. And yes, we're really the Flaming Arrows, and no, we did not come up with the name. Who thinks of this stuff??

while I'm not the biggest fan of k.p. (that's kitchen patrol), at least I'm not at home. Life there is complicated. My dad is in a perpetual bad mood. we all tip-toe around hoping not to set him off. He gets mad about...everything.

usually his bark is worse than his bite, but one time he was so mad at my little brother, he went to hit him...

...but mom stepped in between them.

BOOM!

He put his fist through the wall instead. I try to keep my distance so that I don't get into trouble. I don't think he likes me very much. I'm not sure I like him very much, either.

I love my mom, but I worry about her. She sleeps a lot and doesn't really eat much.

We have lots of talks, and she encourages me all the time, but sometimes she asks me for advice, and I don't know what to say. Especially when she talks about problems with Dad, which happens a lot. And on the rare occasions my father actually speaks to me, it's usually to complain about Mom.

I don't know what it is about me that makes people want to share everything with me. Even here at camp, though I'm not the tallest, or strongest, or coolest, for some reason everyone comes to me with their problems...

Meanwhile, there are the twins, Tessa and Tommy. They are ten years younger than me. Needless to say, we don't have a lot in common. But I do love them very much. Sometimes I feel like I'm a third parent, since Dad works so much. I try to keep them busy when Mom and Dad are fighting. Hopefully the summer hasn't sucked too much for them while I've been away.

Sometimes they'll send me a cute letter...

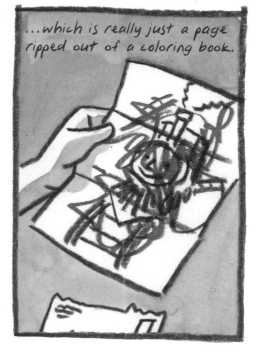

...which is really just a page ripped out of a coloring book.

Aside from the twins, I get a weekly update from my best friend, Violet...

Aug 27, 1995

Dear Aiden,

Well, I have had quite a day. I saw Danny O'Connor at the mall! He walked past me while I was waving, which might be interpreted by some as being rude, but I think he's just being coy. He smells soooo good.

I MISS YOU!!! I wish we could talk on the phone. We definitely need a phone call when you get back home. I bought a calling card so that my Dad won't flip out over another $20 call. Whoops ☺

So it's getting close to the "Big Time": High School! How are you feeling? Have you gone shopping yet for your new high school wardrobe and fun, yet unnecessary, school supplies? I got this set of gel pens that you would die for. Hope your last week of camp is great!

Lylab,
Violet

It is so unfair how quickly the summer went by.

why did Violet have to go and remind me that I start high school in two weeks?

If it's anything like middle school, I am not looking forward to it. I can just imagine high school now:

Big football players punching me in the nads and shoving me into lockers.

medium-sized football players tripping me in the cafeteria and pushing my face into my lunch.

And that one football player with a size complex calling me a

FAGGOT!

at every possible turn.

play a sport.

Okay, maybe not
the sport part.

I'd rather just stay here at camp.
I understand how it works, unlike high school.

PATROL

TROOP

CAMP

Today is Saturday, which means we'll be leaving main camp after lunch for an overnight excursion.

We're canoeing out to Frying Pan Island, which supposedly looks like a frying pan, but we're all certain it looks like a cock and balls.

I love being on the water, cutting across lakes, exploring hidden coves, and breathing the fresh air. It makes me feel very free.

44

45

I know it sounds silly, but not everyone is good at collecting firewood.

It has to be dry.

It can't be green.

SNAP!

And you need all shapes and sizes.

There's kindling—the tiny stuff. You can't just light a match and set a log ablaze. You've got to start small.

kindling

Then there's a range of medium-sized sticks.

medium

Then you've got logs. Of course, split wood always burns faster.

logs

Jacob is our scoutmaster. He's pretty young compared to most other scoutmasters I've seen. I like him. He seems to have an answer for everything.

Hi, Jacob.

And how are we this evening?

Pretty good.

Make sure you all collect some extra firewood for campfire tonight. Ready to sing?

I can't wait!

You've been quiet all night. what's up?

...nothin'.

C'mon, seriously.

Heh. It's stupid. I've been thinking... about melissa.

I figured. wanna talk about it?

why? It's not gonna make her like me again.

Melissa...I...Heh, this is stupid.

No, it's not.

...I think you are the prettiest girl in the world... and I miss you.

You think I'm a JACKASS!

NO, I DON'T. I think it was... sweet. And Melissa doesn't deserve you. One day, you'll find someone who really likes you for being you, not just 'cause you're a football star or whatever.

Thanks, man. I appreciate that.

You know, you're the only guy friend I have who I can really talk to about girls. Thanks.

No prob.

YYYYAAAWWWNNN!!! I am getting sleepy. I'm gonna call it.

'Kay...night.

Night.

59

SUNDAY

Can we make a drawbridge, too?!

Sure, as long as you all find enough wood!

square knot

clove hitch

timber hitch

round lashing

shear lashing

square lashing

diagonal lashing

There is nothing I hate more than shower time. Well, communal shower time, anyway.

ZZZIIIP!!

I like being clean. But I don't want to be seen.

Even when I suck in my belly, I still look pudgy...

...and I have that weird birthmark on my back.

And what if someone thinks my penis is small? I mean, it's not microscopic, but there's the age-old shrinkage dilemma...

Even worse than someone seeing me naked is me seeing others naked. It's so...scary.

:sigh:

I'm so worried that if someone catches me looking at them, they'll think...I dunno, that I WANTED to look...

SSSCCCRRREEEEK

Since today is Sunday, I go to the nondenominational camp service.

I guess it's not technically a Catholic mass, but it'll do in a pinch.

usually I would be serving mass back at St. michael's.

Aiden, are you done preparing?

Almost, Father Danilo, I just have to light the incense.

Then why are you standing about?

I was just, um, looking at this statue of Jesus.

Father, um, why is Jesus's heart on fire?

It is the Sacred Heart of Jesus. You should know that.

...

I feel like, if I keep doing this, I'm getting some extra credit.

Catholicism has a lot of rules. It's hard to keep up.

Sometimes I learn about rules I've been breaking this whole time and never knew existed!

So it can't hurt to have some brownie points in my back pocket.

Father Danilo said I should consider the priesthood, but I don't think I'm holy enough to be a priest.

Also...I want to have sex. Someday. When I'm married. I want to know what it feels like.

I wonder if priests jerk off.

Damnit! So unholy...

Not all funerals are like that.

Looks like this is it. Only the neighbors who found him showed up. Let's get started.

In the name of the Father...

...and the Son...

...and the Holy Spirit...

AMEN.

Go now and spread God's message.

I wonder how many people would show up at my funeral. My family. And Violet. would hardly anyone come? Or maybe it would be like Catie's funeral and all my classmates and teachers would show up. maybe they would cry.

I bet Brad Ledbetter would feel really bad for tormenting me. He'd never say anything mean about me again. I bet nobody would, because that would be a dick move, to say something shitty about a dead person—ugh, sorry, UNHOLY THOUGHTS! Anyway, time to write back to Violet...

90

I met Violet at a Christian camp two years ago. Every summer our family would go to visit friends in the country, and I would go to Christian camp with their friends' kids. People thought I was pretty weird because I was Catholic, but Violet didn't seem to mind.

She was the first person I met who had the same zany sense of humor as me. We would busy ourselves singing spoof songs and consuming huge amounts of candy and soda at the trading post. One time Violet double-dog dared me to sniff some pepper. We were curious if it made you sneeze a lot like in cartoons. Apparently, the cartoons were accurate.

We were inseparable. Until camp was over, of course. She lives really far away, but we became pen pals instantly.

MONDAY

Welcome to orienteering. I'm Ted. I'm really glad you're all here. It's important to know where you stand in the world. Being able to find your way could even be lifesaving in some instances, especially when you're out in the woods.

Everyone bring a compass?

Good. Let's go over a few basic terms...

who here has heard the phrase "find your bearings"? well, in orienteering, we "take a bearing" by...

I'm trying to focus in on what Ted is talking about, but I'm still pretty pissed about what that loser just said to me.

There's magnetic north, and then there's true north. A compass will automatically...

people love pointing out that I'm part Asian, as if I were unaware. It's not always as mean as this guy, but it still gets me upset.

meanwhile, true north actually aligns with the Earth's axis. It's a difference of...

It's always when I'm not actually thinking about how different I am that someone reminds me I'm totally abnormal.

...otherwise, we'll be heading in a completely different direction than we're meant to...

I'm always checking the <u>other</u> box. And I'm so over it.

Okay, everyone, time for lunch. Tonight, read chapters one and two of your merit badge book, and tomorrow we'll start a practice course.

Enjoy eating your hot dog. You probably love eating DOG. Hahaha!

109

And if they were thinking something bad about me...

I could make them pay.

They would be scared of me!

Although, if I were wolverine,

I could trim off my fat

and instantly heal!

screw dieting!

I signed up for basket weaving because I think I'd be good at it.

I've been making hemp bracelets and key chains all summer.

COBRA STITCH

CHINESE STAIRCASE

BOX STITCH

I made matching ones for Elias and me.

It's nice to know that all I have to do is learn one or two types of knots, then repeat that over and over, and in the end you get something really cool. I also already had to learn lots of knots for scouts. I like making them. It's really calming. I figured basket weaving would be the same sort of thing, but with reeds.

Okay, everyone, now that we've looked at some examples and gone over the basics, why don't you head over to the trading post and buy your kits? Make sure you soak the reeds in water overnight so that they're ready for weaving tomorrow.

I thought the whole point of summer was to NOT have homework.

I was kind of curious, why are you taking this class? I wouldn't think that basket weaving is your thing.

It's not, but all the other classes sounded like too much work.

Ha! Wanna go to the trading post with me?

Sure...

uh...what?

well, what I mean is...we were just talking about all these CHICKS...and I think it sucks how Melissa broke his heart. He deserves better.

pfff, Melissa is a stone-cold bitch. Don't worry about Schaefer. He's a freakin' football player, for God's sake. He'll get plenty of tail in high school.

Right, right...How 'bout you?

Actually, you might know her. She went to St. Michael's, too: Sandra Barnes.

SANDRA BARNES!? Reeaaallly?

Yeah, she's friends with my cousin. I am fucking in LOVE with her. I wish I went to your school, just so I could watch her walk every day.

Haha—that's not LOVE, that's called a BONER! Haha!

123

I don't know what to tell you. maybe if you wouldn't cry like a little BITCH all the time, then people wouldn't say that shit to you. If you keep reacting like that, people are going to think you really ARE a faggot. Gotta MAN UP, buddy.

Just forget about it. LET's go.

I know I'm not gay. Gay boys like other boys. I HATE boys. They're mean, and scary, and they're always destroying something or saying something dumb or both. we learned at school how bad homosexuality is. It's a SIN. Gay people do bad things. And I'm not a bad person. I try to do good. All the time. So I couldn't be gay.

And even though I'm not gay, I feel bad for gay people because I know how mean people can be.

I can't imagine what someone's life would be like, you know, being gay out in the open.

Everyone hating you. Strangers telling you they wish you were dead. Parents casting out their own children.

I wish there were no such thing as being gay—then people wouldn't be in so much pain. Including me... for being mistaken as one of them.

And even though I know I'm not gay, I hate that word. GAY. It makes me feel... unsafe.

And worse than that—FAGGOT. I hate it so much. It cuts right through me.

CHOP

CLUNK!

I read in a book once that "faggot" actually refers to a bundle of sticks.

In medieval times, homosexuals were burned alive at the stake. As if they were human firewood. I can't imagine dying like that.

But then, I can't imagine how much hotter the flames of hell would be.

Hey, Elias! where'd you go?

I'm in here with Mark and Bobby.

Hey, guys, whatcha doin'?

Takin' care of "business." Have a seat.

Huh? why is it so dark in here?

can I come in now??

NO! You're too young.

No, I'm NOT!

Fine, but you'll have to prove it.

I will!

I learned about masturbation two years ago. Kind of by accident. Nobody ever told me what it was. One day when everyone was out of the house, I came across a video tape hidden behind the TV. My dad had hidden movies before with dirty scenes, like Fatal Attraction. It was exciting to see boobs and butts. But this time, it was different. I could see...everything. People were doing things that I didn't even know were possible, or even...allowed?

I started watching my dad's porn...a lot...while I was naked. And eventually, I stumbled upon...

...a surprise sensation.

whaa-aa???...
OOHHH!

It felt good, but then I felt really guilty about it. I knew watching porn was against the rules, so this new feeling had to be a sin. And now here I am in this tent full of people jerking off, and I feel like I'm in moral danger.

oh, yeeaah!
oh, baby!

Look out, Cyclops!

SCOTT!

Jean— you saved me!

AAAAAHHH!!!

JEAN! what is it??

TUESDAY

I've always thought archery was really cool. It was obviously invented back in the day by a defenseless nerd like me who couldn't physically defend himself from the bigger bullies at school.

It's important to put a little distance between you and the person trying to pound in your face. Though my method of running away has had its merits...

I doubt it would help me if said bully was wielding a longsword.

I like archery so much that when it came time for me to choose a confirmation name, I chose saint sebastian because his symbol is an arrow, just like my patrol's name.

saint sebastian was a christian in ancient Rome who was tied to a tree and shot with arrows for his beliefs, but he survived.

He went on to do many miracles...until he was beaten to death with clubs, finally becoming a martyr.

Still, it would be pretty badass to pull an arrow out of you and then stick your tongue out at your enemy.

HAK

Sometime this CENTURY, Navarro!

I was very serious about my Confirmation. It's one of the seven sacraments and is kinda like a Catholic Bar Mitzvah. Father Danilo told us how it's just like the Pentecost, when the Holy Spirit descended on the apostles.

It made them all SUPER holy, like Christian superheroes. They all had tongues of fire above their heads, and they could all speak a billion languages to spread the "Good News."

I was very excited to be considered a grown-up christian.

I prayed really hard for the Holy Spirit to make me holy, too.

But when the bishop smeared that oil on my forehead...

...nothing happened.

ORIENTEERING...

Okay, everyone, I hope you all did your homework last night.

I did your mom last night! Heh heh.

Oh, really? I don't think that's true, because my mom did YOUR mom last night, and your mom asked MY mom to tell me to tell YOU to sit down and shut the hell up.

Haha, I like this guy.

I like Ted, too. He doesn't let anyone get away with anything. He always has a funny comeback. I wish I could think on my feet like that. How does he do that?

Good one!

Wow! I did it! I dissed a bully! wait till I write violet.

Speaking of violet, I need to tell her about these dreams. I can't stop thinking about them.

But what will she think...?

what is it with guys and sports? I've just never been into sports.

A bunch of sweaty guys running around tossing balls and trying to score.

And people think I'm gay?

There's a lot of talk about teamwork, but man, if you're not as athletic as everyone else, that word gets tossed right out the window.

SMACK!!

I can't tell you how many times I've been the last chosen for a team in phys ed or managed to botch up what was THE MOST IMPORTANT DODGEBALL GAME IN THE HISTORY OF MANKIND.

or the most important TABLE TENNIS match in the history of mankind.

I also don't want to play today because there's no way I would risk being on the "skins" team. Not only would I botch the most important VOLLEYBALL game in the history of mankind, but my fat would be jiggling all over the place.

I wish I had a perfect body, like Elias.

pecs.

shoulders.

calves.

Biceps.

ABS!!

And...

LUNCH!!!

It's LUNCHTIME! Let's get to the mess hall.

SMACK!

You're SERIOUS? You don't want movies and MTV and someone doing your laundry?

I do miss MTV. But...I'm not excited about high school.

UGH! For real. At least you're going to Lawndale. I'm in the Hillstown south school district. Their high school is the size of a freaking state college.

That actually sounds nice in a way. There are so many people that you can just keep to yourself and be invisible. Lawndale is so small that everyone knows one another's business.

Hey! whatcha doin'?

we're going to start a game of Dungeons & Dragons. want to play?

oooh! what's that?! How does it work?

It's a role-playing game where each player creates their own character, like an elf or dwarf, gnome, halfling, or human, and then there's a quest that they all go on and fight in epic fantasy battles.

So, like acting out LORD OF THE RINGS??

NO. It is NOT Lord of the Rings. Every game is its own unique story as told by the Dungeon Master. Do we really have to include people who have never played?? They're going to slow us down.

Everyone who wants to play can play. They'll figure it out.

So, I'm just tryin' to help out is all. why you gotta act like...you know... DIFFERENT?

I'm not ACTING like anything. I'm just doing whatever it is I do. I don't know how to be the way everyone WANTS me to be.

I mean, you talk different, you walk different. I'm just sayin', life would be a whole lot easier for you if you were just more...

more what? NORMAL?

Yeah! NORMAL.

WEDNESDAY

I don't think you're aiming high enough.

First of all, loosen up.

:KICK:

You've gotta aim JUST above your mark, 'cause the arrow doesn't fly straight, there's a little bit of an arc.

Good moooooorning, miss maaaary.

I wish I were cool like Ted. He's different, but in a good way.

Maybe I just need to update my look.

Something bold that says "I'm different AND cool!"

Hey, guys, what's up?

206

Holy. Fuck.

Come on.

what the HELL did you do?

what did I do? I just lost a TOOTH, asshole!

Aiden wouldn't just knock out your tooth. You DID something.

why does he need to be so different? It's like he's always trying to get people's attention. It's EMBARRASSING.

You're a real ASSHOLE, Mark, you know that?

SO WHAT?? That kid is gonna have his ASS handed to him next year if he keeps that shit up. I'm trying to get him ready. Time to MAN UP.

They can be pretty fun.

I'm not great at all of them...

...but some of them I'm actually pretty good at...

...if not the best!

But we all worked together...

...and won!

225

CLICK

I'm kinda freaked out about it.

You ARE? Why?? You're so popular.

Pff, no, I'm not.

But you're on the football team.

I'm on JV. And I have nothing in common with the jocks. I just like playing ball. They all say shit about me 'cause I have long hair. Meanwhile they all wear Abercrombie and think Limp Bizkit is good music. Total douchebags.

HAHAHA! Oh no—that's horrible!

THURSDAY

255

Heard about that counselor they let go?

Unbelievable.

I actually think it's ridiculous that they let him go. For what?

We can't risk having PEOPLE LIKE THAT around our kids.

Who says this guy's a pedophile? So someone found out he's gay. So what?

You've gotta be kidding me! Scouting volunteers shouldn't be talking about anything sexual at all.

Come on, you're being a HYPOCRITE.

HOW?

You're LYING if you're telling me that none of us have made a dirty joke or even just talked about guys and gals in general.

TOTALLY DIFFERENT!

I agree.

This guy's a PERVERT. He could be teaching things to our KIDS. He could have TOUCHED some of them, and they're too afraid to come forward!

This Ted guy wasn't saying or doing anything sexual to the campers.

Someone found a personal letter and outed him.

Because he didn't do anything wrong. For all we know, he's just doing his job.

That we KNOW of!

I don't understand why you're defending this guy.

No. Scouting doesn't allow HOMOS. It's SICK and IMMORAL and is prohibited in the bylaws, thank GOD. And it's gonna stay that way.

267

271

Mail call!

Actually... I'm not feeling well. Can I go to bed?

what's wrong?

I think it's just something I ate.

Hello?

Hi, Tessa, it's Aiden.

Hi, Aiden! I miss you!

I miss you, too. Can I talk to Mom?

Ummm... Mommy and Daddy are fighting.

Sigh. Right. Will you tell her... that I love her?

Okay!

It's just going to keep going like this forever...

...on...

...and on...

...and on...

...and on...

...and on.

TOO SHORT.

TOO FAT.

Not MAN enough.

Not WHITE enough.

Not STRAIGHT enough.

I'll never be safe ANYWHERE.

I can't.

FRIDAY

I...I'm just so TIRED. I can't DO this anymore! I'm WEAK.

I AM NOT WEAK!

WHOOSH

AAAAHHHH!!!

KICK

You were looking for me?

well, we didn't know where you were, and I was worried, so...

Yeah, well, we all were...

oh.

I'm sorry I freaked out. You just...you just took me by surprise there.

Mail call!

Navarro,

This is for you.

I...I thought there was no mail today!

I said a BROOM push-a-moppa push-a-moppa push-a-BROOM!

uh-huh! okay! one more time...

VALLEY GIRL STYLE!

No. It's okay.

It takes a lot to put out a fire. You have to constantly douse it with water.

The water cuts off the fire's air supply, basically strangling it.

when the fire is finally overwhelmed, the flicker will go out.

But there are still the hot coals underneath, which are actually even hotter than the flames.

You have to completely submerge the coals to make sure they're out.

Scout regulation states that a fire has to be "hand-touch" out before leaving it unattended.

But sometimes, even when you think the fire is out...

...you're wrong.

My life feels like a mess. There are people I still don't know how to deal with...

Goodbye

...a family I don't know how to live with...

...and there are feelings inside me that scare me to death.

But today I discovered...

...this fire isn't done burning.

AFTERWORD

This book is a work of fiction, and yet much of it is based on my personal experiences. I grew up in scouting from a Tiger Cub all the way up to an Eagle Scout and Assistant Scoutmaster. There are many things I am grateful for. Scouting got me outside. It taught me how to work with others. It gave me self-confidence. It was a way to meet people who did not go to my school. I made friends. And though I don't see those people for years at a time, when I do, that bond is still there.

However, there were experiences I had during my time in the Boy Scouts that were very hard as a closeted kid. Over the years, the Boy Scouts have become more inclusive of sexual orientation and gender thanks to people in and out of scouting who made their voices heard. But when I was a kid, it was not okay to be gay. In 1995, the year in which this book is set, gay and queer people were routinely villified, ridiculed, and hated. Fear of AIDS only fueled the bigotry. Back then, gay adult scout leaders who came out were immediately removed from their post. Though scout bylaws have become more inclusive, homophobia still exists in many troops today, because homophobia is nationally and internationally a systemic issue.

Like my character Aiden, I felt overwhelmed by this culture of hatred. Also like Aiden, I once kneeled in a camp chapel with a knife against my wrist. I wanted my anguish to stop. I wanted to silence my fears. I was so scared of high school that I thought I would not survive it. Worst of all, I hated myself. But like Aiden, I found the strength to live. And although living is scary when we continue to suffer, I would do it all over again to be able to write this book for you. To hope. To dream. To want love. These are dangerous acts. Fear and hope are bound up together inside of us, alongside our flaws and our divinity. In this darkness, we can find an inner light to guide us. And there is light in you, even if you can't see it.

Mike Curato

RESOURCES

While my journey has led me far away from that chapel on a hill, I have known some dear people who did not survive. Their loss is a void that can never be filled. And they give me strength to say these things to you.

If you or someone you know is contemplating suicide, ask for help. Call the National Suicide Prevention Lifeline at 1-800-273-8255.

There is also TrevorLifeline, 1-866-488-7386, for specifically LGBTQ support.

Coming out is hard. For resources to support you in your self-discovery, go to thetrevorproject.org and glsen.org.

ACKNOWLEDGMENTS

I want to thank . . .

my editor, Laura Godwin, who has always believed in me and who cheered me on when I wanted to try something I've never done before.

my agent, Brenda Bowen, whose love and support have seen me through the best and worst of times, in writing and in life.

my assistant, Sabrina Montenigro, whose hard work and diligence helped make this book happen. I am forever grateful for the endless hours of scanning that I did NOT have to do.

my art director, Mallory Grigg, and designer Colleen AF Venable for helping me make this book look spectacular.

Tara Hardy, the first person to read my rough ideas. Thank you for saying "Yes, you do need to make this, and yes, you can."

Lynda Barry, whose Writing for Artists workshop gave me the confidence to take on such a huge project.

my fellow authors/illustrators for their time and incredible advice: Samantha Berger, Ruth Chan, Brian Selznick, and Sarah Jane Lapp, and all the support from Molly Burnham, Jarrett Krosoczka, Grace Lin, Lisa Yee, Dave Roman, and Craig Thompson.

my other dear friends, of whom I'm blessed to say I have too many to list here. You know who you are. I don't know where I'd be without you.

my old friends from Troop 37. I can't express how much our time meant to me. Our troop was the first group of people I felt accepted by. I can't smell a campfire without thinking of you. I miss you.

my family, for my mother's unconditional love, for my father's hard work and sacrifices, for my sister and brother's laughter.

Lara Robbins, my real-life Violet, to whom this book is dedicated. Thank you for showing me the power of friendship. You saved my life.

and Dan, for everything.

WITHDRAWN
PUBLIC LIBRARY
BROOKLINE

WITHDRAWN
PUBLIC LIBRARY
BROOKLINE
PUTTERHAM
PUBLIC LIBRARY OF BROOKLINE
959 WEST ROXBURY PARKWAY
CHESTNUT HILL, MA 02467 8/20